The Secret Of
Friendship

Williona Butler

Friendships can be made when two hearts are being brave.

Transferring to a new school turned my whole world upside down but I tried to stay positive without having a frown.

Being a new student was hard to trust because I didn't know anyone and that was hard enough.

To my surprise new friendships were made just by me sitting down and not being afraid.

I started making promises that I knew I couldn't keep and found myself friendless in under 2 weeks.

This feeling didn't feel good and it surely wasn't fun, so I was back at school feeling all alone.

Kids wanted to fight and argue with me too but I walked away feeling upset and had no clue.

I tried to understand what the problem was about and went to the teacher to figure it all out.

It was clear change had to be made, so I gathered all my new friends and let them know I was sorry and felt ashamed.

This feeling that I felt finally felt good because I owned up to my mistakes just like I should.

I'm glad I have these friendships in the kindness they have shown me because it made me a better person in the friend I want to be.

"Remember to always be yourself because that's who people connect with"

-Williona butler

The End

Made in the USA
Middletown, DE
07 May 2022

65448335R00015